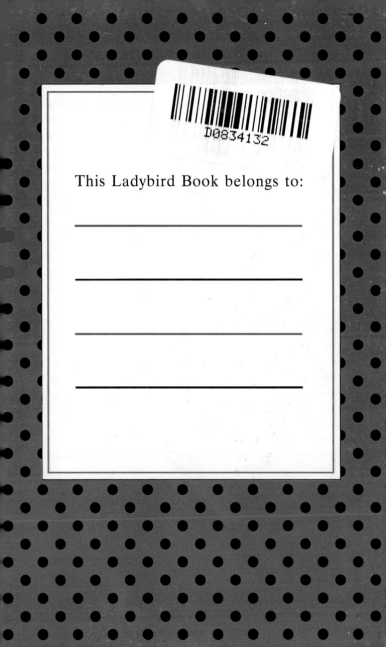

This Ladybird Book belongs to:

_____

_____

_____

_____

D0834132

All children
have a great ambition …
to read by themselves.

Through traditional and popular stories, each title
in the **Read It Yourself** series introduces children to
the most commonly used words in the English
language (*Key Words*), plus additional words
necessary to tell the story.
The additional words appearing in this book are
listed below.

Robinson, Crusoe, parents, storm, waves,
crashed, swam, island, called, raft, cut,
ready, calendar, stick, each, goats,
clothes, ragged, skins, umbrella, picked,
near, corn, growing, bread, pots, Friday,
English, speak, worked, washed, helped,
wanted, lit, running, waited, seen, working

A catalogue record for this book is available
from the British Library

Published by Ladybird Books Ltd Loughborough Leicestershire UK
Ladybird Books Inc Auburn Maine 04210 USA

Robinson Crusoe

adapted by Fran Hunia
from Daniel Defoe's original story
illustrated by Robert Ayton

When Robinson Crusoe was
a boy, he wanted to go to sea.
His parents would not
let him go.

"There are so many dangers
at sea," they said.
"Stay here with us.
You will have more fun here."

Many years went by. At last
Robinson Crusoe was a man.
So he ran away with a friend
and went to sea on a big ship.

Robinson Crusoe liked the work
and made some good friends
on the ship.

Then one day there was a big storm.
Big waves crashed down on the ship

and he was sad that he had
run away from home.

"After this, I will go home
and stay there," he said.

Then a big wave crashed
on to the ship!
It washed Robinson Crusoe
off the ship and into the water.
He swam on and on.

At last he came to an island.
He walked up the beach.

The next day, Robinson Crusoe
went to look for the other men
from the ship.
He shouted and shouted
but no one was there.

He looked out to sea and saw
his ship. He swam out to look for
his friends but no one was there.

Then he saw the ship's dog and two cats. "You can come with me and be my friends," he told them.

Robinson Crusoe saw many things that he wanted. He made a raft to put them on. Then he called the dog and cats and they all went back to the island.

Robinson wanted to go out
to the ship again the next day,
but the storm came up again.

A big wave crashed on to the ship
and Robinson Crusoe saw it go
down into the water.

Now Robinson Crusoe knew
that he would have to stay
on the island.

"I must get to work and make
a good house," he said to himself.
He cut down some big trees
to make his house.

He worked hard for days and days,
and at last it was ready.

Robinson Crusoe was pleased
with his house.

Then he said, "I must make
a big fire, so that it can be seen
from a ship and they will know
that I am here."

The dog helped him to get the fire
ready. Now all he had to do
was to light it when he saw a ship.

I came ashore here
September 30th 1659

"I must make a calendar
so that I know how long
I have been here," he said.
"I will get a big stick,
and put one cut on it each day."

Then he wanted to have
a good look round his island.
He saw some goats on the beach.

"If I can get a goat," he said,
"I can have some milk."

All day he ran up and down
after the goats. At last
he had one big goat
and two little ones.

Now he could have lots of milk.

As the years went by,
Robinson Crusoe's clothes
were more and more ragged.
He had to make some new clothes
from goat skins.
After that he made an umbrella
to keep the sun off as he worked.

He was pleased
with his new clothes
and his umbrella.

Robinson Crusoe was working
near his house one day,
when he picked up a bag
that had come from the ship.
Some corn fell out of it.
Some days after that, he saw
something growing.

"This must be corn," he said.
"I will water it and look after it.
It would be nice to have
some corn to make into bread."

Robinson Crusoe made some pots
like the ones he had made
when he was a boy at school.

He put them in the fire
to make them hard.
Now he could keep the milk
and corn in the pots.
He was very pleased with himself.

One afternoon Robinson Crusoe
looked up and saw a ship!
He ran up the beach
to light the fire.
Then he waited for the ship
to come and get him.

But no one on the ship saw the fire.
Robinson Crusoe shouted
and shouted, but it was no good.
The ship went by.

By now Robinson Crusoe
had been on the island
for many years. He had goats
and corn and a good house,
but he had no one to talk to.

"I must make a boat
to take me away from here,"
he said to himself.

So he cut down a big tree
and made it into a boat.

It was hard work,
but at last it was ready.

He tried very hard
to get it to the water,
but it would not move.

One day Robinson Crusoe saw
a footprint. He could see that
it was not his footprint,
as it was too big.

"Who can have made this footprint?"
he asked himself. "There must be
someone here on my island.
I will have to find out who it is."

Then he saw some men
with little boats
down by the water.

One man was running away
from the others.

Robinson Crusoe said to the man,
"Come with me. I will help you."

The other men ran away.

"As it is Friday,
I shall name you Friday,"
said Robinson Crusoe.
"You can stay with me
for as long as you like."

Friday went home
with Robinson Crusoe.
He helped milk the goats,
water the corn
and make the bread.

Robinson Crusoe was pleased
to have a friend to talk to.

One day Friday came running
to the house.

"Robinson," Friday shouted.
"Come see. Big, big boat."

Robinson Crusoe ran down the
beach and shouted. He lit his fire.

The men on the ship saw the fire.
They let a boat down
into the water, and went to see
what Robinson Crusoe wanted.

Robinson Crusoe and Friday
got all their things
and put them on the ship.
Friday wanted to go too.

Robinson Crusoe was pleased
to be going home at last,
but he was sad to go away
from his house, his goats,
his corn and the island
that had been his home
for so long.

LADYBIRD
READING SCHEMES

Read It Yourself links with all Ladybird reading
schemes and can be used with any other method
of learning to read.

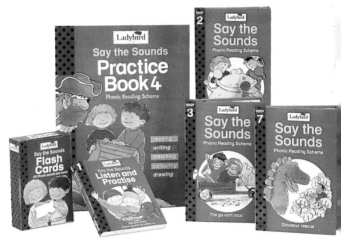

Say the Sounds

Ladybird's **Say the Sounds** graded reading scheme is a
phonics scheme. It teaches children the sounds of individual
letters and letter combinations, enabling them to tackle new
words by building them up as a blend of smaller units.

There are 8 titles in this scheme:

1 **Rocket to the jungle**
2 **Frog and the lollipops**
3 **The go-cart race**
4 **Pirate's treasure**
5 **Humpty Dumpty and the robots**
6 **Flying saucer**
7 **Dinosaur rescue**
8 **The accident**

Support material available: Practice Books, Double Cassette pack,
Flash Cards